The Knight Dark Era

Jake Triulcio

I'd like to dedicate my first ever published novel to my family, who have encouraged me to pursue this hobby into a career, and for supporting me along the way.

Contents

CHAPTER 1

Ore

Levda; a world full of magic, and mysteries. A world full of heroes, and legends. Adventurous it may be, but even this wonderful world had its darkest hour – the Dark Era that happened one hundred years ago.

Despite our efforts, I know it shall return to the world of Levda. I can sense it. It's close, and I must be prepared for it.

Fifteen years ago, I set out to journey through Levda. From the highest mountain in the island kingdom of Jalvan, through the scorching desert kingdom of Sa'vero, to the ancient ruins of the past. I have meditated, fought, learnt new spells in the animal kingdom of Verosa, and made my mind and body strong. Making the energy of my aura powerful.

I'm ready to face the challenges that will scar the world once more.

My journey takes me to the outer rim of Jalvan, an island south of The Capital. It's known for its peaceful serenity, with farmlands, a small town, and wild boars that roam northwest of the island's rocky terrain. A place for those who wish to live simple lives as farmers, or hunters.

Up on its tallest mountain, I rest by the edge of a cliff, staring at the sunset. I take a deep breath, feeling the gentle breeze on my skin and blowing through my spiky silver hair. I listen to nothing but the wind that twirls around the mountain. The spirits of the dead whisper into my ears.

The wind settles, and the shout of a young adventurer fills my ears. I turn around to see a seventeen-year old boy swinging a wooden sword around, training himself to become a strong warrior.

I call out to him. 'Ghost, are you ready to head back to town? The sun will set soon, and you've been training for long enough.'

He keeps swinging his sword, excitement in his eyes. 'Just a little longer, Ore. I want to do a few more hours of training so I can be ready for our travel to Jalvan City.'

'I'm well aware of your motivation to improve yourself every day, but even a warrior must learn to sheath their weapon, and rest.'

But he doesn't listen to a word I say, and he points his sword at me. 'I want to duel with you,' he says with a smirk on his face.

I laugh at his challenge. 'Come now, Ghost. Do you expect to win this time? It's true that every sparring match we've had you've grown stronger, and your skills have improved. But even with all those years you've put into training, you're still no match for me.'

But without hesitation he charges at me with full force, his sword to the side, and swings it. I jump in the air and dodge his attack, then counter with a wind spell to blow him away. Ghost tries to stand his ground, but he struggles to fight my spell and goes flying to the wall.

I summon out my staff, grey wood with a black orb on top, with roots securing it into place. 'I warned you, Ghost. Now to finish you off and drag you back to town.'

I whisper an incantation and charge my staff with a fire element, just enough to knock him out. But before I can finish, Ghost charges at me again. This time he channels his aura into his sword and jumps in the air, his wooden blade pointing down, overflowing with a yellow flame.

'Ultimate …!'

By the way he holds his weapon, I realise what Ghost plans to do. He plans to overwhelm me with one of his strongest techniques, but he has forgotten where we are.

'Hold on, Ghost, that's a terrible idea!'

I jump off the cliff as Ghost finishes shouting out his move.

'… **earthquake!**'

His sword stabs into the ground, creating a shockwave that shatters the cliffside. This is possibly one of the most reckless things Ghost has ever done; and I recall a long list of reckless actions he has made over the time we spent together.

As we fall from the mountain, and with Ghost's screams filling the air, I remain calm and think of a plan to save us. I quickly point my staff to the ground and summon a twister to catch me. Then I point and cast a spell of levitation on Ghost.

'**Float!**'

And I catch him along with the falling debris. I hold firmly to my staff to keep my spell active and slowly lower Ghost down, close enough for me to release the spell and run to safety. I drop to my knees and turn my head to see the pile of rubble that could have buried us.

Ghost is laughing.

'Stop being so reckless,' I say to him, catching my breath. 'Your actions may lead to our demise.'

But he keeps on laughing, and replies with a smile. 'No promises.'

I should have expected him to say something like that. I'll let it slide for today.

I get up and brush off the dirt from my robe. 'Let's head back, Ghost. We must rest up for tomorrow.'

'Sure thing, Ore.'

We head back to town, and plan for our journey to Jalvan City.

***

The moon is full and shines brightly in the sky. I'm sitting on the rooftop of an inn where Ghost and I have been staying for the past few months, right above our room. I can't sleep, and it has nothing to do with the events that happened today.

It's something else, something dangerous.

I stare up at the moon, close my eyes, and allow the moonshine to rain on my body. Feeling the cool gentle rays. But that feeling suddenly goes dark. I open my eyes and sense something foul. It's coming from outside of town, along the road to the north. I jump off the roof to investigate.

Hurrying out of town, I come across an old house on the side of the road, completely burnt out and abandoned. The porch is covered in ash, the yard withered. I see bouquets of flowers and writing on the fence, but the writing is hard to read and the flowers have all dried up. A foul aura is coming from the house; it brings a horrible memory that leaves a scar, forever a wound for this peaceful town.

I recall my first visit here as if it were yesterday. It was a most unpleasant experience, with so much sadness that once flowed around this town. Ten years ago, this house went up in a blaze. Two lives were lost that night. One survived, but in a state of shock that took them years to recover from.

As I visualise the horrible event, I hear a woman's voice in my head. It's telepathic magic, and there's only one person I know who can use it. The one being I haven't heard from since the Dark Era.

'Such a tragic time for someone so young. Wouldn't you agree?'

I speak out loud so she can hear me. 'Yes, it has been. But I've done my part to save him. I assume this was your work?'

'Why would I ever hurt a poor soul who means everything to me? Do you think of me as a beast that would prey on such an innocent child?'

I clench my fist. 'Yes, you are.'

A dark mist appears around me, and from the mist comes a deep black shadow. I stare at it but remain calm. The shadow points at me. *'You think I am heartless. You dare say such a thing to a powerful sorceress?'*

'Just because you're immortal doesn't mean you're powerful. Now, I suggest you leave before I decide to strike you down, E'va.'

'I'd like to see you try.' E'va's shadow launches at me. I dodge her attack and charge up an orb of light from my hand.

'Taste the burning light that shall rid you from this world. **Guardian's light!**'

I throw the orb at E'va's shadow. In an instant the shadow disappears, with her parting words echoing into my ears.

'You may have grown stronger, Little Wizard, but that won't change the fact that the boy will be mine.'

The mist disappears, and the silence of the night returns. I speak aloud, suspecting that E'va is still close by, watching me.

'I've prepared myself for fifteen years. I wield the power that you will submit to. For it is my life's goal to learn all the knowledge this world has to offer, and stop you!'

I raise my head to the sky and claim victory, but only from a mere shadow. I wonder if E'va's grown weaker over the past century. But now is not the time to think about it. Much time has passed since I left Jalvan City; for me, with the blood of an immortal, time fades from one's mind.

I feel weary, and head back to the inn for a night's sleep.

CHAPTER 2

Ore

It's early. I'm comfortable in my bed. Although the sun is out, I refuse to get up because I had been sleeping so soundly.

But a loud adventurer outside of the inn won't let me sleep peacefully.

'Hey, Ore! Wake up already. Let's get going. I'm ready for our trip to The Capital.'

Crawling out of my bed with the blankets wrapped around me, I approach the window with my eyes barely open. Ghost is outside, waving his arms with a big smile on his face.

I gently rub my left eye. 'Ghost, it's still too early to go. I'm too tired to travel, and have yet to check my inventory. Can we hold out until the afternoon?'

'Come on, you can do that on the way,' he says, yelling like a child. 'I want to head out right now!'

I'm still half asleep, and there's no way I can rest and check my inventory with Ghost bickering all morning.

I yawn and come up with a plan to keep him busy. 'I just remembered a key potion ingredient, which is crab eyes. I think you should try and get some sea crabs along the beach. I won't have enough time to do that, so could you go kill some? Thirty should do it.'

Ghost quickly pulls his wooden sword out and points it towards the beach. 'No problem. I'll slaughter them real good.'

'Hey, don't forget about the eyes,' I yell out to him before he goes too far to hear me. As soon as he's out of sight, I go back to bed and curl into a ball in my sheets. That should buy me about five hours, since the sea crab's eyes are very fragile. Ghost will most likely bring about ten. I gently shut my eyes and catch up on my rest.

Unfortunately, for the next twenty minutes my mind won't stop. I toss and turn in my bed until I can't sleep anymore.

'Damn. Why did you have to wake me up, Ghost?'

I jump out of bed, put on my black robe, and head on downstairs into the inn's dining room for breakfast. The innkeeper greets me with a smile.

'Well, good morning, Ore. You're up earlier than usual.'

I sit by a table that's close to the fireplace. 'Yes, I do enjoy waking up early in the morning after doing some late-night research,' I reply sarcastically.

She laughs. 'Oh, has our town's youngest adventurer caused you some trouble again?'

'I would go back to sleep, but unfortunately my mind won't stop racing. Anyway, I'll have the inn's special please.'

The innkeeper wraps her apron around her waist and heads over to the kitchen. 'One order of eggs and roasted boar steak with sunwheat seasoning, coming right up.'

I remove a pouch that's hanging from the side of my robe, and place my hand inside. It sinks into the dimension I created for the sole purpose of storage while I'm on the road. Inside are things I've collected, like potion ingredients, magic tomes, history books, and a boat with a magical wind enchantment on the sail. I withdraw the materials I've gathered from this area, and count one by one to see if there's enough.

'Let's see here. Two dozen boar tails, eight boar horns, fifteen black mountain roses, thirteen sea crab's egg sacs, and twenty deep sea pearls. Yes, that should about do it. I can make some experimental potions with these. Plus, Creem will have a field day with the pearls.'

That reminds me – I forgot to send her a message. From the pouch I bring out a lily pad with a fairy flower attached to it. The flower opens up, with a little fairy bud gently waving side to side. I speak clear to the bud with an image of Creem in my thoughts.

'Good morning, Creem. It's been quite some time since I updated you on my current location. Well, right now I'm on the outer rim of Jalvan, and I plan to make my return hopefully before nightfall. Oh, I forgot to mention something special – I managed to obtain those deep-sea pearls you always wanted. I can't wait to see you again. Not a day goes by without me recalling your beauty.'

The flower closes up and spits out the fairy bud, allowing it to fly out the window and towards The Capital. After that I begin to smell a lovely aroma from the kitchen, and out comes my breakfast. The scent of the boar steak flows throughout the dining room. I quickly put everything away, and the innkeeper places my food in front of me. The wheat seasoning is scattered on the steak, dancing around the hot surface.

'I hope you enjoy it,' says the innkeeper as she walks away.

I grab my fork and knife and dig straight in, enjoying each bite of the steak. When I finish, I hear Ghost calling out to me.

'Ore, you ready yet? I got some crab eyes like you wanted.'

Satisfied with my meal, and now fully awake for the journey, I grab my pouch and go outside. Ghost stands beside a big pile of crab eyes.

'Did you collect all of that by yourself?' I ask him, my eyes following the pile from top to bottom.

He smiles, and nods. I'm amazed how much he has. He might have destroyed their entire species. 'I remember what you showed me a few months ago; how to collect their eyes. It's super easy.'

He says this even though it's only his second time collecting them.

'You amaze me, Ghost. It's as if you improve quickly from just doing something for the second time, and at a shorter time period.

Anyway, everything is all sorted. We are all set to head out.'

Jumping in the air with excitement in his eyes. Ghost and I collect the crab eyes, and begin our journey.

'Time to start our adventure!' he screams out to the town.

***

As we walk along the road to a suitable place to sail out, we come across the burnt house. Ghost pauses for a moment and takes a good look at it.

I stop. 'Take your time.'

He brings out his wooden blade and thrusts it right in front of the yard. He drops on one knee with tears flowing from his eyes.

'Thank you, Mother, Father. For everything you've done for me. I promise you. I'll become a great adventurer.'

Saying his final farewell to what used to be his home, and leaving behind his wooden sword, we set out to Jalvan City.

CHAPTER 3

Ore

The morning breeze from the sea is salty but refreshing, and the waves rock the boat gently. It's a wonderful day to sail to Jalvan. It's nice and peaceful out on the ocean. No storms for miles and no sea monsters to ambush us. Even if I enjoy this moment, my friend here certainly isn't feeling the same. Resting his head on the side of the boat, staring out into the sea, moaning.

'Ore … I'm bored.'

'Ghost, you need to enjoy yourself at times like this – even though an adventurer must always be on guard when they are traveling. There are times like this where we must learn to calm our minds, and take in the beautiful scenery.'

He ignores my advice and continues to moan. 'All I see is sea water, clouds, and the blue sky. What's to take in?'

Oh, how I wish Ghost wasn't as stubborn as a drunken man demanding another bottle of ale.

'I'm going to take a nap. Wake me up when we reach land.'

'I'll make sure to do that.'

Ghost places his hands behind his head and lays down. He immediately goes to sleep. I guess killing those sea crabs this morning must've been exhausting for him. I wouldn't argue about that. I mean, Ghost used a wooden sword. It takes a lot of power just to break open their armoured shell with one of those.

Free from his whining, I return to absorb the atmosphere. I close my eyes, taking advantage of this peaceful moment. But I realise that it's too quiet, even for the sea. I open my eyes and notice the boat remains still. The enchantment on the sail is still working, yet it's as if time has suddenly stopped.

'It seems that you're finally leaving that boring island.' The voice echoes in my head, which only means one thing.

E'va.

'Stopping time just to finish the job? I must say, it's unlike you to resort to using a spell like this only to kill me.'

Her shadow appears before me, floating above Ghost and leering at me. 'Why would I ever fight you in this state? Even if I tried, I'm unable to do much.'

I search around, but I don't see her body anywhere. 'Where are you hiding? How are you able to communicate with me if you're not in range?'

'Why would I share my secrets? Besides, I'm only here to chat with you about my dear little adventurer.'

I wish I could be rid of her, but unfortunately, I can't do anything while she remains in that form. I make my stand, staring at her shadow. 'I have nothing to say to you, so I suggest you disappear and never bother me again.'

E'va's shadow swirls around me and speaks closely to my ear. 'Why must you be so cold to me? I do cause so much pain on this land, but they deserve it. You don't understand how much pain I was in when I first came to this world.'

I face her. 'I do understand. It was painful at first, but all of it has changed. People can change, and so can you. After all, I know everything there is to know about you.'

E'va tilts her shadowy head in confusion. 'Oh?'

'Your origin, your pain, your sacrifice. But even with all of that you couldn't save the very being whose blood is the same as yours.'

She slowly backs away from me. Though she's silent, I can sense her anger. My words are like daggers, striking her in the heart.

'How dare you?' she bursts out in anger. 'How do you understand me? No mortal can understand my pain.'

I laugh. 'You honestly think I'm a mere mortal? Please, even you must be able to figure out what I am from everything I just said. Or has your madness clouded your judgment?'

E'va lashes out at me with a furious gravitational force, weighing me down. I hold my ground, though the pressure is quite overwhelming. I assumed E'va couldn't use any powerful spells while in her shadow form, but that turns out to be false.

'I'll find out who you are and burn you in the dark flaming abyss, Little Wizard.'

Her shadow disappears, along with the gravitational force, and time flows back into the world.

'The truth will surely burn you more than it will me,' I say.

I sit back down on the boat, and think about my next move. E'va has been more active as of late, and that worries me. The disguise enchantment I cast on myself seems to be holding, but it won't be long now before she strikes. Have I grown stronger than her? Am I able to defeat her? What plan does she have that could cause harm to this kingdom again? These questions weigh heavily on my mind, and the only thing I can do now is wait.

***

We arrive on the shores of Jalvan in the afternoon, stretch out our legs, and prepare to move forward. I open up my pouch and allow it to shrink my boat, sucking it back inside. Then we journey along a path leading into the forest.

As we walk along the road, I begin to wonder what E'va's plan is for when we arrive at the city, or if she even has a plan. I look at Ghost and notice a smile on his face, a bright and cheerful look from someone who has always wanted to become an adventurer, and is now living his life's dream. I pray that his life can continue without any hardships that could destroy him physically and mentally.

We arrive at a small town that is in a terrible state. Broken barrels, windows boarded up, and the smell of blood in the air. Dark mist looms about, obscuring the ground beneath our feet. I sense something foul here, but I'm not sure what it is.

'What happened here?' Ghost asks.

'I'm not sure. Perhaps it was a bandit raid?' I can sense the residents hiding within the buildings, as if they're afraid of something. What I can tell from this sensation is that this wasn't a bandit raid. It's something more sinister, and there's only one person who fits into all of this.

'Ghost, allow me to take care of this.'

As I take a step forward, Ghost reaches out and grabs my shoulder. 'Are you sure about this?' he asks, concerned.

I look over to him with a smile. 'It should be a simple task to clear the area.'

He lets go of my shoulder, and takes a step back. 'Okay, good luck then. I'll be here if you need me.'

I move slowly to the centre of the town with my eyes closed, my staff out. I begin to feel the eyes of ferocious beasts staring at me and pause for a moment. With my hand on top of the orb, I speak an enchantment.

'I call upon a spearhead of light that shall pierce the heart of darkness.'

The spearhead of light appears from my orb, and just as I'm prepared to fight, an evil shadow rushes me from behind. I quickly duck to let it fly past me, and stab it in the head the moment it turns around.

My eyes widen at the sight of my enemy. I can't believe it; a wolf cloaked in darkness, an ancient beast. I assumed they all went extinct after the Dark Era, but that thing wasn't alone. I hear growling all around us, and I shout out to Ghost. 'Brace yourself. We're surrounded.'

'Wait, what?'

I sense another wolf leering at him, ready to attack. 'Behind you!'

The wolf launches at him but Ghost dives to the side, away from its bloodstained fangs. Guarding Ghost, and trying to focus on the beasts will waste time and energy. I can't do this alone.

I clench my right hand. 'I call forth a blade drenched in the aura of the dead. **Phantom blade!**'

From my right hand, a sword with the souls of the dead flowing from it appears, and I toss it to Ghost. 'Quickly, Ghost. Use this.'

He catches it and dispatches the wolf that charges at him. 'Thanks, Ore. Okay, time to slaughter them.'

He roars and lashes out at the foul beasts around him. I do the same, and twirl my staff through my fingers, taking them out one after another with the spearhead until their corpses lay by our feet. Ghost cheers for our victory, but I sense the battle has only begun.

CHAPTER 4

Ghost

I cheer loud like nothing can stop me. Those stupid beasts can't handle my awesome skills. But Ore starts yelling at me.

'Ghost, this isn't over. Stand your ground, and never let your guard down.'

I don't understand why he wouldn't be happy for our victory, but I do listen to him, and focus. Though I'm not sure what else there is to fight.

But suddenly I sense a powerful aura in the mist. I've never felt something like this before. Then I hear a loud howl, but not like the wolves we took out. 'Ore, what the hell is that?' I yell.

But he can't hear me over the howling. My eardrums feel like they're about to explode. Then the loud howl goes silent, and out from the mist comes a large beast, striking Ore with its giant claw and sending him flying into one of the houses.

I stand firm and face the big beast. Its head resembles a wolf but its body is large, standing tall on two legs like a human. I've never seen such a beast. *What the hell is it?*

The beast charges at me. Stunned by its form, I can't move my feet or shield myself with my sword.

Why can't I move? Why am I frozen in place? I need to kill this thing right now, or else ...

As the beast raises its claw, I suddenly see images in my head. Memories of a house engulfed in flames, and a monster cloaked in fire.

I'm afraid. I'm afraid to fight it, but … but … I must do something, or else I'll die by this monster, and never fulfil my promise.

'Don't lose focus, Ghost,' I hear Ore shouting, and he appears in front of me with his staff blocking the beast's claw. 'You're stronger than this werewolf, though it may seem powerful and ferocious. That doesn't mean it's invincible. Snap out of it, and fight like a true adventurer.'

The werewolf tries to force its way through, and uses its other claw to knock Ore out of the way. But he holds his ground and keeps it away from me. His words snap me to my senses, and give me the will to fight. I hold tightly to my sword.

'Thanks, Ore. You sure know how to motivate me.'

I charge at the werewolf and thrust my blade into its chest. It roars in pain and backs away from us, covering its wound.

'Alright, ugly. It's time to take you out. Ore, cover me.'

'Understood. I believe I shall use a spell to heat things up. **Hell's barrage!**'

Fireballs appear in front of Ore, and he hurls them at the werewolf. With the beast overwhelmed by Ore's spell, I come charging at it, ready to swing my sword as hard as I can. Charging my aura into my blade, I shout, '**Ultimate…**'

I swing my sword at it and release the aura concentrated within my blade. '… **strike!**'

A direct hit with my weapon sends the beast a few feet away from me. The werewolf tries its hardest to get up but struggles to stand, and coughs up blood. I walk over to it with my blade, ready to finish it off.

'I can't die today. I've just started my adventure, and I won't allow my fears to block my path.' I close my eyes, ready to swing my blade again. '**Blind strike!**'

In an instant I rush past the beast with my blade swung to the side, and its body splits in two. The mist fades away and the town is free from the darkness. I fall to my knees, trying to catch my breath, taking in the sound of the wind.

'Ghost … are you okay?' I feel Ore's hand on my shoulder.

I turn to him with a smile. 'You're right, Ore. I really need to take in the peace and quiet.'

He laughs, and pats my back hard. 'Oh, how I dreamt for this day to come.'

I stand up, and stare out into the sunset. 'My first step to become a great adventurer. It feels so overwhelming.'

'You'll get used to it, Ghost.'

We hear a crowd cheering us. The villagers are coming out from their homes, running up to us, thanking us for saving their home. They wish to throw a celebration for our good deed, but we can't stay any longer.

Well, I didn't want to stay any longer. We return to the road.

***

We continue our travels through Jalvan Field in the middle of the night. The road is barely visible, but Ore casts a spell on his staff, and lights up a path for us.

'It sure is dark isn't it, Ore?' I ask him.

'Indeed. If it weren't for that werewolf, we would have arrived at Jalvan City before nightfall. But such misfortunes tend to happen from time to time.'

He has a point. What are the chances of coming across a town with horrifying beasts like those wolves, and that big werewolf creature? *Where did they come from? What reason do they have for attacking the town, and why do they exist?*

These questions are driving me crazy. I wish an answer could just fly into my mind now.

'Curious about those creatures? Well, I could tell you about them, if you wish.'

'Ore … did you say something?'

He looks at me, confused. 'What do you mean, Ghost? I haven't said another word to you.'

'Then where did that voice come from? Was it my imagination?'

'Voice?' Ore stops walking. I turn around and see him facing to his right with his staff pointing off into the distance. 'Ghost,' he says, 'stay close to me, and take no heed of that voice in your head.'

What's he talking about?

I don't understand. But the look in his eyes tells me that something bad is about to happen. 'Can you be a little clearer? What's going on?'

Then I hear that voice again. Only this time, it's not in my head.

'Such a protective wizard. I merely offer to answer his enquiry about my creations.'

Purple flames appear out of thin air, and standing at the centre is a person wearing a black robe, their face covered by a hood. Holding out their hand to me, they say, 'There's no need to be afraid. I'm only here to answer you.'

I don't like this. A stranger appearing out of nowhere, telling me not to be afraid. The way Ore is reacting only means one thing – this person is dangerous.

I walk behind Ore and ready myself to fight.

'I don't know who you are,' I say as I point my finger and start acting tough. 'But I'm certain that you're a dangerous person. I trust Ore enough to know that you're lying.'

The mystery person raises their hand, and then slowly removes the hood; revealing themself to be a woman with long black hair, and blood red eyes.

'My name is E'va, and I've been waiting for this very moment just to see you.'

'E'va?' *Why does that name sound familiar? And why do I get the feeling that I've seen her before?* I don't recall ever meeting her, yet my soul says otherwise. 'Who are you, and what do you mean you've been waiting to see me? I've never met you before.'

I try to walk forward but Ore stops me from taking another step, and turns to face me. 'Don't heed her words, Ghost. They'll poison your mind and leave you vulnerable.'

'Ore …'

I've never seen him like this. It's as if he's a completely different person, but he's right. I feel weak all of a sudden, just by staring into her eyes. 'Thanks, Ore. I needed that.'

He smiles and hands over an orb with a spiritual aura flowing from it. I grab it and it transforms into the phantom blade. Wielding the sword with confidence, I ready myself to take on this mystery woman.

But she doesn't seem happy about my response. Her shadow flames start to grow more furious.

'You dare wield that weak blade to your mistress? Is this the kind of response you give to someone you loved once?'

E'va grabs one of her flames and throws it at us. Ore casts a spell to shield us from her attack.

I charge at her, and swing my blade. 'I don't know what you're talking about. Why would I love you? I already have someone I care about.'

She laughs at me while dodging my attacks. 'Ha, I bet she doesn't feel the same for you. She's probably already forgotten you.'

Her words make me angry, and I feel the need to kill her. 'Don't you dare say that about her. We made a promise.'

E'va grabs another one of her flames and it hits me. I get pushed straight into Ore, and lay on the ground by his feet in pain.

'Are you alright?' Ore asks while he places his hand on me. 'I won't allow you to continue with this madness, E'va. **Bolt!**'

Ore shoots out bolts of lightning from his staff straight at her, but she blocks his attack with one of her flames. 'Is this all you wield? Pathetic. **Black shards**!'

From the sleeve of her robe, E'va throws shards that hit Ore on his left leg and right arm. He falls to his knees and tries to stand up, but he looks as if he can't move. E'va laughs at our defeat, and walks over to us.

'Such a weak Little Wizard. Those shards won't allow you to move at all. You're like a fly trapped in a spider's web. Just waiting to be eaten. Now I shall take your life, and claim what is rightfully mine!'

Something snaps inside of me. I don't know what it is, but it makes me feel powerful. I slowly get up from the ground and grit my teeth. 'You plan to kill Ore? And dare speak about the girl I love? I'll make you regret saying those words.'

A spark of fire flows around my body and I know my eyes have started shining red like a wild beast. I roar and charge at E'va. My mind goes blank and all I can hear are screams. A few words are spoken but I can't make any of them out.

I slowly lose consciousness, and the only words I hear clearly before passing out are, 'I won't allow this to control you, Ghost. I'll find a way to cure you.'

CHAPTER 5

Ghost

I'm in a strange forest, lying by a tree with a stab wound in my right arm. There's a book in my left hand and a dagger by my feet. I reach for it but my body won't budge. I'm low on aura, and I can feel my soul fading away.

'Dammit, I need to get out of here before …'

Then a rift from the ground opens up, and slowly ascending from it is E'va, looking very angry. Her gaze sends a chill down my spine, with sweat dropping down from my head to the ground.

She reaches for my dagger, and uses her dark magic to enhance it.

'You'll remain in a frozen state till the day you die. This will be your punishment for disobeying me. I pray your next life won't cause me so much trouble. Farewell … Lobia.'

E'va thrusts the blade through my body and pierces my heart. The pain is unbearable, and I scream out the last ounce of my breath as I'm being turned into stone.

My heart races as I sit up, drenched in sweat.

What the hell was that about? I quickly check my body and find no stab wound, or any kind of wound. Not even a scratch. *Was I dreaming?*

I sit up and find myself on a couch inside a living room, with a blanket covering my legs.

'Ah, you're finally awake.'

I look to my right and see Ore sitting by a table, sipping from a cup.

'I'm glad you're safe for the time being. Last night was certainly …
unexpected, and eventful.'

'Last night?' I only recall fighting E'va, and that Ore was about to
die. But I don't remember anything else.

'What happened, Ore? Did I do something reckless again?'

He takes another sip and slowly places his cup on the table. Then
he takes a deep breath. 'Reckless is hardly the correct word for our
situation. I'd say you went insane like a wild beast. It's been such a
long time since you lost control of yourself.'

Now I remember. I suddenly had this blazing aura flare up from
inside of me, and I couldn't control it. I recalled having this feeling
when I was a kid. But it was so long ago I could barely remember
the details.

I lower my head. 'Sorry for making you worry about me, Ore. I just
need to control my anger.'

'You shouldn't put yourself down like that. After all, it was E'va's
doing. She pushed you beyond your limit without any knowledge
about your berserker state. She disappeared immediately after you
burned her. But I had some trouble trying to calm that temper of
yours.'

I stand up from the couch, and sit by the table in front of him. I
realise that his left cheek is burned, along with his right arm and left
leg; both are bandaged up. 'I hope I didn't hurt you.'

He waves his hand. 'I'm fine. It's only a burnt cheek. Though I
wish I'd suffered less injuries. E'va was the one who did most of the
damage. I struggled to get you to the city. Fortunately, I was lucky
enough to reach the city's gate, and ran into a few guards on duty.
They helped us into my house and alerted the medical centre to
treat our wounds.'

'I see. I'm happy we made it to Jalvan City. Although I wish it was
in better shape.'

Ore nods, and gently places his left hand on his injured one. 'Yes, as do I, but let's not allow last night to ruin this moment.'

Ore's right. I'm finally here, and ready to make a name for myself. I can imagine my life here. Running around the fields taking on monsters on wanted posters. Exploring caves and ruins, becoming a great adventurer.

Full of excitement, I jump off my chair and hurry to the door. 'Come on, Ore, let's go explore the city.'

'No!' he shouts, then continues more calmly. 'I mean … Creem says I must allow my injuries to heal, and I know better than to go against her orders. So I'll be home all day.'

I briefly wonder why he reacted like that, but I don't think about it much further since I'm really excited to go sightseeing. 'Well, I'll head out then. Rest up.'

***

I casually walk around, exploring the city. The people here seem happy, enjoying their daily lives. It reminds me of my childhood. My father used to take me on his patrol around the residential district. Such wonderful memories. I wish to relive that joy now.

My stomach begins to growl, and I go searching for a place to eat. The only place I come across is a café right next to a park. I walk in, and a young waitress greets me.

'Welcome to our humble café. Please follow me to your table.'

I follow the waitress to an empty table, right next to a group of people who look like adventurers. I'm surprised to see them at a place like this. One of them has short white hair that covers her right eye, and is wearing a blue coat with a hood pulled over her head. She's enjoying a slice of cake. The other two must be from Sa'vero; they are big and muscular, one with scales on his left arm, the other with scales on his right. They look similar, wearing chausses and greaves. They boast about some big beast they took out in their homeland.

The waitress offers me a glass of water and a menu. I thank her with a smile. She leaves me to choose what to eat, although it doesn't look to be my type of food. I observe the café and notice how colourful it is. There are pots of flowers by the door, paintings of trees and gardens, and a few relaxed customers enjoying their meals.

Ore's right about enjoying the peace and quiet. It really is relaxing. I slouch down on my chair and take it all in. But all of that changes when a group of men storm into the building with their swords out. One of them pulls out a pistol and fires it in the air.

'Everyone, stay where you are. This is a robbery.'

The customers and workers start to panic, but the gunman shoots again and growls at them. 'Keep it down, or else I'll put a hole through your skulls!'

His threat silences the entire room.

'Good. Now, I want you all to empty your pockets. Coins, jewellery, even weapons that could fetch a hefty price in the black market. My boys here will be bringing a sack to you, so you better cough up or else you'll die!'

I sit still for a moment. *Who the hell are these guys? And what makes them think I'll do nothing at a time like this?* I try to stand up, but for some reason my legs won't move. It's as if they're frozen in place.

I try to move again but then I hear a voice in my head.

'I knew you might try and do something stupid. Thankfully, I'm great at reading people's expressions. Your intention is to be a hero, rather than submitting to a threat.'

I notice the adventurers next to me staring at the thugs like a pack of wolves stalking their prey. The one who was eating cake turns her eyes towards me.

'If you wish to take them on, I suggest you join forces with us, and we shall deliver justice.'

I can only assume that she's a mage, though I've never experienced this type of magic before. I'm unable to move a muscle in my legs, but I smile at her to indicate I'm agreeing to help. The two men prepare themselves; one slowly puts on black gauntlets, while the other places his hand on an iron mallet by his chair. We wait for the thugs to spread out. One of them walks over to me, pulling a sword from his belt as he comes closer. 'Alright, kid. Cough it up.'

I distract him with a question. 'That's an interesting sword you got. Mind if I borrow it?'

He looks confused, then starts laughing – only to have one of the adventurers swing the mallet into his face, knocking him out. The sword flies through the air and pierces my table. The other robbers notice the commotion and the gunman points his pistol at me. He grins and pulls the trigger, but an adventurer steps in front of me with his arms raised up to his face. The bullet hits him, but it ends up reflecting back at the gunman, hitting him in the shoulder. As the gunman falls to the ground, I pull the sword out from the table and quickly knock out the remaining thugs one by one. I thrust the blade to the floor and let out my victory roar.

'Yeah, that's it! None of you guys stand a chance against me.'

I keep cheering until I see an ice shard come flying close to my head. I look behind to see it hit the gunman, who has his gun pointed at me again. He falls to the ground with blood gushing from his forehead.

'You keep your guard down and assume you claim victory without analysing your enemy. This behaviour will kill you, and you will be known as a nameless novice.' The mage pointing her finger out. She gently blows on her pointed finger, and continues to speak. 'But thankfully I've saved you from that. You seem to have some skill as a swordsman, but too lax. Even after a fight.' She smiles. 'But since the danger has been dealt with, how about we invite you for a drink at the Traveller's Tavern?'

The two big adventurers start flexing their muscles behind their companion, and I accept their invitation.

CHAPTER 6

Ghost

A crowd of adventurers cheer for an encore from a band of traveling bards. The beats of the bongo drums, the heavenly sound of the flute, and a beautiful voice from their singer fills the room. I'm sitting with the group of adventurers who invited me. We raise our tankards and clink them against one another. We laugh, and sing along.

'I'm so glad I ran into you guys back at the café,' I shout, my face red from the ale I've drunk. 'It's been a long time since I took out a group of bandits. I feel like a true adventurer, though I wish I took them to the barracks instead of the guards.'

One of the muscular men pats my back with a powerful force that pushes me close to the table, a grin on his face. 'You did well, little fella. It's a good thing Sherva stopped you when she did. Or else we'd never get the jump on them.'

She blushes, hiding her face behind her tankard. Then she tilts her head back to drink what's left in it. 'It was nothing. I only prevented this novice's mistake.'

As I finish another round of ale, I say, 'We never actually introduced each other. I'm Ghost, and I plan to be a great adventurer.'

The two big adventurers get up from their chairs, and flex their muscles.

'I'm Basto, the man with a mighty fist.'

'And I'm Gasto, the man with a mighty mallet.'

Then Sherva gets up and removes her hood. A pair of cat ears pop out and twitch as she starts to speak. 'And I'm … I'm … Sherva. The Wi-Wise …' She leans forward to pose with her companions, but ends up losing balance and falls back onto her chair. She manages to finish her sentence. '…wise mage of the group!'

Basto and Gasto laugh. It seems Sherva can't handle her alcohol. I laugh along with them as she rests her head and dozes off. Gasto continues with a laugh.

'To finish our introductions, we're known as the Silver Coin. With my twin brother Basto's enchanted gauntlets and my iron mallet, we protect anyone from danger. Even our little Verosian mage here, while she casts her spells on any foe.' He wields his mallet in the air as he boasts.

I try to clap in praise of them, but my hands keep missing each other and I end up laughing about that. 'You guys are awesome. I can't wait to be as cool as you. But I'd rather go solo. Tag along with a few adventurers every now and then, and then go our separate ways.'

Basto pats my shoulders and smiles. 'I like the sound of that, Ghost. As long as you keep venturing out and meet others along the way, you'll live your life to the fullest.'

We call out to a waitress for one last round and call it a night. Basto picks up Sherva, who is talking in her sleep, and we head out through the front door. We wave our goodbyes, and leave in opposite directions.

Walking through the quiet streets, my eyes are barely open as I struggle to find Ore's house. I'm still smiling even as I swerve side to side.

'Okay, now … where was Ore's house again? Did he move? That's crazy, how can he lift a house?'

A group of people emerge from the shadows. One of them pushes me, but I manage to stay on my feet.

'Hey, you. Are you the one who caused my brothers some trouble?'

I look at them, and tilt my head. 'Huh? What are you talking about? If you mean the guy who tried to steal my boar leg from the tavern, then yeah, that's me.'

I get pushed again.

'I'm talking about our brothers who tried to rob a cafe this afternoon.'

I take a moment to think clearly, but I just can't. One of them points at me and starts shouting.

'Yeah, I think this is one of those adventurers who killed our ace gunman, and put our brothers in jail. I saw them when I was keeping watch around the area.'

Now it comes back to me. 'Oh, you mean those jerks in the café.' They keep on spouting this and that, but I can barely understand them. 'Who the hell are you? I don't have time for this, I've got to get back before my friend scolds me for being out too late without him.'

I try to walk past them, but I'm thrown to the ground. I can barely hear a word coming out from the man's mouth, but I do hear the words 'kill you'.

'Why would I kill you?' I ask. 'You've never done anything to piss me off.'

They all scream at me, 'No, you drunken idiot. We're gonna kill you.'

I understood that at least. 'Oh, kill *me*. Well, I'll have to kick your arse all over the city then.' I stand and put up my fists, but my eyes begin to blur. I close them and hear their shouts.

The ground starts shaking. I open my eyes to see vines popping up around me. They wrap themselves around the group and slam them to the ground. I don't understand what's going on, but I don't care. I try to take a step forward but I trip and fall onto something soft.

'Well, you certainly had too much to drink, young man,' I hear a mysterious woman say.

Then a familiar voice adds, 'Ghost, you better explain this to me immediately. But first, I would appreciate it if you remove your head off of my wife's breasts.'

I try to open my eyes as I stand straight. 'Oh, hey, Ore. I was just … just …' I try to walk over to him, but I trip and fall again – this time to the ground. Too comfortable to move, I just fall asleep.

***

I lay on the grass in the middle of a forest with my sword by my side. I stare into the trees and watch the leaves fall on me. It's peaceful, like a dream.

Yet it isn't. I feel as if this world is real.

'Knight, come forth. I require something from you,' says a voice from above.

I sit up straight and look up at a tree behind me, and see a being who's as beautiful as a dark rose sitting on a large branch.

'Of course, Mistress. I shall be up there in seconds.' I grab my sword and leap up to the branch beside her, and kneel. 'What do you need, my lady?'

She brushes her long black hair and points over to a group of butterflies. 'Those bugs were flying around my face. They are annoying. Dispose of them.'

I lower my head. 'As you wish, Mistress.'

With my blade I swing and release a powerful force that shreds their wings.

I turn back. 'I've fulfilled your request.'

She laughs as they fall helplessly to the ground. 'You've done well, Knight. I shall reward you when we return to my fortress.'

I smile at her, and kneel before my mistress again so she can climb on my back. We jump off from the tree. When we land, a little boy comes running towards us through the trees.

'Big sister, I found the fairy elves' village. Maybe they can help us?'

She pats him on the head. 'Well done, O'va. I'm proud to call you my little brother. Now we can bring my dream into reality.'

O'va smiles, and hugs his big sister. 'I'll always be here for you, no matter what, big sister. I'll do my best to become the best wizard, and never leave your side … E'va.'

I hear her name echo in my ears, and then my mind goes blank.

CHAPTER 7

Ghost

I'm tossing and turning in the morning with a killer headache. Fragments of my memory are missing from last night, except for the fun time I had drinking in the tavern with a group of amazing adventurers. I also recall a strange dream, similar to one I've had before, except that I was a completely different person.

What does this all mean? What is it trying to tell me?

I sit up and realise that I've been sleeping on Ore's couch. I guess I found my way over here from the tavern. I look around and notice a woman sitting by the table reading a book, sipping from a teacup. She's wearing a red dress with flower patterns that run down from her shoulders and twirl around the dress. Her red hair forms a twin tail loop around her pointy ears.

I try to speak but my headache prevents me from saying a word. The woman notices that I'm awake and walks over.

'I was wondering when you'd wake up. You must've had too much to drink last night. My darling was worried and went looking for you. Of course, I wouldn't allow him to go alone since he's still recovering from his injuries.'

When she mentions injuries her face suddenly goes from bright and cheerful to dark and scary. This woman now looks like she would kill you in cold blood.

'Wait right here. I have something that'll take care of you. It will be swift, and painless.'

Her tone sends a chill down my spine as she turns and heads into the kitchen. I better sneak out in case this woman is a stalker who snuck in here. I get up from the couch, but a potted plant beside it sprouts out and wraps around my body, throwing me back down.

'I said to wait right there,' she shouts, returning with a bucket and a small towel, and placing them in front of me. I see green nectar that looks as if it's been boiled in lava. She places the towel in it and lets it soak for a few seconds, then places it on my face.

I brace for what promises to be the most painful death I'll ever experience. But I don't feel it burning; it's warm and soothing, as though I'm standing in a garden feeling the gentle rays of the sun. It slowly cools down, like a gentle breeze blowing away the pain. The woman pulls the towel off my face and smiles.

'There, now – that wasn't too bad?'

The chill I felt earlier is gone and my warrior spirit flares out from me. I jump up and start stretching out wide.

'Man, that felt good. I feel like I can take on an army of boars and run around the kingdom.'

'My goodness, you're energetic! My husband wasn't exaggerating about that.'

'Husband? Do I know him from somewhere?' I scratch my head.

She laughs. 'Why, it's Ore of course. Who else would live here?'

The shocking answer leaves a shocked expression on my face. I thought this woman was a stalker, but she's Ore's wife!

She bows and introduces herself. 'My name is Creem. I'm the head of the medical department here in Jalvan, and …' Creem blushes, and hides her face behind her hands. '… and I'm Ore's wife. I always get flustered whenever I say that.'

She clearly loves him a lot if just saying she's his wife makes her react that way. But speaking of Ore …

'Um, Creem, would you know where Ore is right now?'

'Oh, that's right. My darling wanted me to tell you that he'll be in his lab down in the basement. He wishes not to be disturbed, and will forget what happened last night if you stay clear from the lab.' She points over to a door next to the stairway.

'Last night? I don't remember anything.'

She giggles. 'I shouldn't expect you to remember. It's alright, it's best to forget about it.'

'I do recall having a strange dream.'

'Dream?'

'Yeah, only this time I was someone by the name of … Knight? Last time I was Lobia, and now Knight. What does it all mean?'

Creem looks concerned about this, but then she hides it with a smile. 'Perhaps it was just some wild dream. Nothing to think about.'

'But the strangest thing is that E'va's in it, and for some reason I feel like I've seen that little boy before. His name is O'va.' I continue to think about that dream, and wonder if Ore knows anything about it.

Creem offers me some advice. 'Maybe we should save it for later. Ore has told me about your strange dreams, and we can work on it tonight if you wish.'

'Um, sure, okay. I'd like to get some answers as soon as possible, and Ore couldn't help me out on his own. He only made some theories that make no sense to me.' I sit back on the couch, my mind settled on the matter. But I recall something very important. 'Ah crap, I forgot! I spring back up and hurry out of the house.

Creem chases after me to the door. 'Ghost, wait. Where are you going?'

I wave to her as I continue running. 'Sorry, I forgot there's something for me to do today. I'll explain when I get back.'

***

Rushing through the crowd and jumping through side roads, I arrive at a very memorable place. Jack's Arms, a well-known blacksmith in the kingdom; a place I used to visit almost every day when I was a child. I recall Jack hammering dense from my father's equipment, throwing magma rocks in his furnace, and fixing up a full set of armour for me. It's been almost ten years since I last visited, but the wait is over.

I walk in, ready to yell out to Jack, but someone is arguing with a large man with scales on his shoulders that run down the side of his arms.

'Look, Boon, I keep telling you that I can't sell this weapon. I've been working on it for a long time. It's part of the set of armour I forged, and I ain't parting with it.'

'Come on, Jack. At least tell me what material you used to forge such an amazing sword.'

'It's a trade secret. Your only chance of knowing the material is to fight the person who was supposed to wield it.'

They keep arguing until Jack notices me standing by the door.

'Oh. Sorry, young man, I didn't see you walk in.' He brushes off the man he was arguing with and focuses on me. 'Welcome to Jack's Arms, best blacksmith in Jalvan. What can I do ya for?'

I waltz on over to Jack and jump on his counter, a smirk across my face. 'I just came over to do this.' I tilt my head back and slam right onto his forehead.

He falls back but keeps his balance, and slams his head right back at me. Then we collide our heads and push against one another.

He grins at me. 'Only one little runt has the balls to headbutt me.' Then he gives me a big hug, crushing me with his strength, laughing. 'It's good to see you, Ghost. It's been too long!'

I start to feel every ounce of my breath escaping from my body. I start to gasp for air. 'Jack … can't … breathe.'

He loosens his grip and gives me a second to catch my breath. 'Sorry, kid. I'm just so happy to see you again after what I heard. The report says no one survived, so I thought you'd be dead. And also …' He pauses for a second and scratches his head. 'I'm sorry about your parents, as well.'

I stay silent for a moment, but I brush away that emotion and put a smile back on my face. 'It's alright. I'm happy to see you too, Jack, after so many years. I'm here for that equipment you once promised.'

'Ah, right. I'll be right back.'

Jack heads into his storage, leaving me alone with the man. I notice him staring at me.

'So, you're the one who's supposed to wield that sword. When I saw Jack polishing that blade, I thought to add it to my collection.' He holds out his hand. 'My name is Boon, Jalvan's number one mercenary.'

My eyes start to sparkle, and I quickly shake his hand. 'You're a mercenary? I heard about your guild from my father. You guys work really hard to stay on top around here. Not even the adventurer's guild can keep up.'

He grins. 'Yeah, it's a great guild, but that's only because I'm the strongest among the rest. I take on high-class bounties, and go on jobs that the princess herself issues.'

'That's so cool. I want to do work like that, too.'

'Well, you'll have to train hard to even stand on that level of work.'

I grin at him and point straight at his face. 'Then how about a duel? To prove to you how strong I am.'

Boon summons an iron mallet out of thin air, slams it to the ground, and points it at me. 'You're on!'

Jack had returned to the counter with my equipment and overheard the challenge. He flexes his large arms and yells, 'Alright, a duel!

A perfect chance to test the endurance of this armour. Let's head outside, fellas.'

Jack hands over my new gear and we walk out of his shop with a spark of rivalry flaring between me and Boon.

CHAPTER 8

Ghost

Jack roars out in excitement for our duel to begin right in front of his shop. While Boon stretches, I fit myself into my new armour and toss over my old leather set to Jack. I feel completely different in it, able to move more freely than in my old gear.

'Wow, it fits perfectly! Thanks, Jack.'

'I knew you be the same height as your old man when you grew up, and I kept it nice and shiny. I wouldn't dare to give up a masterpiece to any random traveller. Now, pick up your sword and see how it feels.'

I wield my weapon, expecting it to be heavy, but it feels just as light as my old wooden sword. And the length of the blade is about my height.

I face Boon and ready myself to fight. 'Okay, let's get this duel started! I want to see how well I can do with my new equipment.'

He laughs. 'Nothing will change, kid.'

He charges at me with intense speed and swings his mallet. I barely dodge his attack and back away from him. Boon rests his mallet on his shoulders with a smug look on his face.

'Not bad. Your reflexes are sharp, especially at that speed. But this mallet does have a disadvantage, so I'll lighten things up for myself.'

In an instant his mallet disappears, and appearing in his hands are two daggers. It's the second time I've seen him summon out a weapon, and it's much faster than Ore summoning the phantom blade.

'How are you summoning your weapons? I've never seen someone make them appear so quickly.'

Within a blink of an eye, Boon charges at me. I jump back to gain some distance but he immediately catches up, and tries to stab me with his daggers. I manage to block his attack with my sword, but I feel an immense force coming from Boon's attack. His aura is strong, possibly stronger than mine. As we push against each other, Boon grins at me.

'This kind of summoning is quick and easy. All I have to do is think of the weapon in my head, and it will appear before me. This'll work on any weapon with a magical seal I placed.'

He charges again, rapidly swinging his blades at me. I dodge, block, and parry his attacks. But I'm struggling to keep up with him, and eventually I end up tripping on my own feet and falling to the ground. *Dammit, he's too quick to keep up with.*

Boon rushes towards me again, with his arms stretched out and his daggers pointing at me. 'This is gonna leave a scar on your body, kid. There isn't any metal in the world that these daggers can't cut through. **Dragon strike!**'

He increases his speed and aims at my chest plate. His daggers hit the mark, but instead of piercing through, they shatter before his eyes.

'What the …?'

I take this moment to swing my sword at him and send Boon a few feet away. I look at my armour; not a scratch on it. I'm amazed how durable it is.

I look over to Jack. 'You've done a good job, Jack. I really love this armour.'

He laughs, proud of his work.

I face Boon, who's still in shock about his daggers shattering. 'How is this possible? My blades are the strongest, forged from the fangs of an elder dragon. There's no metal that can break it.'

'Wrong, Boon,' yells Jack. 'There's one type of metal that can shatter it. A rare material that no one can find – not even the miner guild in Sa'vero can find it. But one man did the impossible, and gave me the honour of forging the strongest armour for his own son. The mighty Knight ore.'

Boon's eyes widen. 'You're joking? Knight ore … Knight ore!'

While he's distracted, I take the chance to use one of my techniques. I ready myself to sprint, and shout out, '**Ultimate acceleration!**'

My body starts to feel light as air and my movement is much faster. I charge at Boon.

'I'll finish this off with one strike. **Ultimate …**'

Boon quickly refocuses on the battle, and summons out his mallet again to counter. But I am too fast for him to react in time, and swing my sword as hard as I can.

'… **strike!**'

My blade connects, and Boon takes a direct hit. He pauses for a moment with his head down, then slowly takes a step.

'Damn, kid. You're one hell of a warrior,' he says as he plummets to the ground.

I swing my sword to the side, take a deep breath, and stare up at the sky. 'You're not too bad yourself.'

My first duel in Jalvan City, and I came out on top. I respect Boon's strength; he deserves his reputation as the strongest mercenary, and I hope to work with him from time to time. I feel my adventure has just begun, and I can't wait to see what else this world has in store for me.

I sheathe my sword and walk over to Jack, but I suddenly feel so weak and a shroud of darkness covers my eyes. Jack's voice echoes as I fall.

'Ghost! Ghost, you okay?'

My body feels numb, and my mind is slowly fading.

Where am I going? Why can't I move, or see?

I keep repeating these questions until I hear E'va's voice answering.

'It's because your soul is within a state that can finally accept the void. But your heart refuses to fall in. Don't resist, just let go of what you have and accept what you're meant to be. The darkness is your home, your power. I can offer you a far better weapon than what you have in your possession. Just come find me, in the Shadow Cave.'

What does she mean a far better weapon? She must know something about me, something Ore would never say. I refuse to fall into the void, but I still want answers. With my aura suddenly up in flames, I battle the darkness and force my way out.

CHAPTER 9

Blake

It's early morning in Jalvan. The streets are quiet, and many people are still asleep. I march through the streets towards the residential district to fulfil a request from the princess of the kingdom. I stop in front of a house, knock on the door.

'Ore, this is General Blake. The princess requires your assistance on a personal matter.'

'Come on in, General.'

I enter the house but don't see him. Creem is there drinking tea with a young man chowing down on a big boar drumstick.

'Good morning, General,' Creem says as she places her teacup down. 'How may I help you?'

'Good morning, Creem. I've come to make a request to Ore on behalf of the princess. Is he around?'

She stares at a door by the stairway. 'Unfortunately, Ore has been working tirelessly for the past few days, ever since he returned from his journey. I checked on him this morning and found him sleeping on the floor. I believe he should rest.'

'I see … that's unfortunate. Very well, I shall inform the princess and hope we can—'

The young man leaps from his chair. 'I'll do it!'

His eyes shine brightly for adventure, and his energetic behaviour speaks of a young man who's eager to work. Not only that – I feel as if I've met him before, but I can't possibly think where.

'Very well, young man. I shall fill you in on the assignment as we head off to meet with the princess. But first, may I ask—?'

Again, I am interrupted. This time it is Creem.

'I refuse to let him leave this house. He collapsed yesterday, and didn't wake up until late at night. All I could hear from him was the void, and darkness. I will not allow him to venture out without curing him.'

I don't quite understand what's happening, but if Creem is worried about this young adventurer, then I can't ask him to come. Even if I do, she would simply revert to her frightening behaviour, and I wish not to live through that again – not after my last injury when I was a lieutenant.

'I understand your concern, Creem. I'll make sure the princess is aware of Ore's condition and proceed without him.'

The young adventurer moans like a child, and goes to sulk on the couch. I feel bad for him, but you can never disobey Creem's orders. I bow to her and take my leave, and make my way to the city's gate.

Ten minutes into my walk to the gate, I sense someone watching me.

A spy hiding in the shadows? No, I felt this sort of presence before. One I thought to never feel again.

I stop. 'There is no point in hiding. My senses have grown stronger over the years … Ghost.'

Jumping off a rooftop is the young adventurer from Ore's house. 'Wow, you actually caught me. And here I thought I'd gotten better at hiding from you, Blake,' he says with a smile across his face.

I laugh, happy to see him again. 'Well, many experiences of you hiding around the military district back when you were a child gave me the idea to work on that.'

Looking at Ghost, I recall a time when I was a young man myself. I had recently been promoted to lieutenant, under the command of the greatest general of Jalvan, General Drake – the man who saved Jalvan from a corrupt cell within our military ranks, and brought peace to the kingdom. I was inspired to be just like him, a true hero to the people. During those times I learnt a lot from him; from maintaining the strength of our troops, to learning a few of his ultimate techniques. Though challenging they may be, there was one lesson that proved to be the most difficult of them all.

Babysitting his son, Ghost.

Full of energy, and wanting to go on adventures, he usually ran off somewhere while on patrol with me. I chased after him every time, and ended up in either a fight or forced to play hide and seek with him. Though I found it quite stressful, seeing that smile made it all worth the effort. I even remember the times I sparred with Ghost, teaching him proper stance and fighting techniques. Though he didn't follow any of my instructions, and attacked recklessly.

I close my eyes. 'Ghost, I'm very relieved to see you alive after all these years. I feared the worse after receiving the report about your father.'

I open my eyes and see him looking sad. 'Yeah, I guess you can say I was lucky. But would you call it luck if you lost everything?'

'I can understand how you feel. I grieved for you and your parents. They were all good people.' I feel sad for him, but though I feel the pain inside of me, it can't compare to how he must feel.

He smiles. 'But right now I want to try and become a great adventurer. My parents wouldn't want me to sulk for the rest of my life, so I need to get back up and fight on.'

Just seeing him like this lifts my morale. I raise my hand and clench it. 'Yes, let us move forward and never allow sorrow to hold us back.'

With a rekindled spirit, we head down to the city gate.

***

We stand outside the city, waiting for the princess and a few more who will be joining us for the journey.

'Ghost, I assume you've turned seventeen?'

'Yes, several months ago. Ore said we wouldn't come back here until I turned this age. I'm so happy to be here, and happy to see you again, Blake.'

'Have you been keeping up with your training?'

'You mean killing big werewolves and being awesome?'

I sigh. 'Come now, has everything I taught you meant nothing?'

'Of course it means something. Every time you try to teach me, I get to spar with you.'

I should've expected him to say that. 'Well, I think the princess has strange taste in men who think recklessly.'

'Hey, I may be reckless, but I'm not strange,' he says angrily. 'Speaking of her, is she actually going to come along too? I thought you'd hate having her wandering around.'

'Yes, I can understand what you're thinking. But rest assured, as long as she travels with me and a few guards, I'm happy to take her anywhere. And with you along for the ride it will only make me feel more comfortable. Even if you are reckless.'

Even if Ore isn't coming, I'm happy that Ghost gets to come along. He and the princess once shared a bond that could only be described as love. Ever since they were children they played in the castle's garden; Ghost would play as a hero, while the princess plays as a damsel.

'Morning there, General. I hope I haven't kept you waiting.'

I turn to the gate and see a mercenary I've personally hired. 'Ah, you've made it. Glad to see you take on the job, Boon.'

He swings his iron mallet to the ground. 'I'm always up for a job request from you, General. The payment is good and I get to travel with the princess. The boys back at the guild are probably jealous of me.'

He notices Ghost standing next to me and runs up to him, wrapping his arm around his head. 'Well, if it isn't Ghost, the man with the unbreakable armour, and a powerful aura. Did the general offer you a job? Well, having you around will make things more exciting.'

I watch him swing Ghost around while Ghost taps on his arm to let go, like they've been best friends for a long time. 'I had no idea you knew Ghost, Boon. When did you two meet?'

'I met him yesterday, we had an amazing duel. This kid sure showed me. I can still feel the impact he gave me.'

I'm impressed. Ghost managed to defeat Boon, Jalvan's most powerful mercenary. It makes me wonder how much he'd improved since I last sparred with him. Just as Boon lets go of Ghost's head, a few guards approach with horses, and following them is the princess in her brightly shining golden armour.

I kneel. 'Good morning, Princess.'

She smiles at me. 'A good morning to you too, General. I hope everything is sorted for our journey.'

'Unfortunately, Ore is unable to come with us. But I have his replacement.'

I point over to Ghost, who then waves at her in high spirits. 'Hey, Jessica. Long time, no see.'

The guards pull out their weapons at Ghost's lack of respect.

'Stand down,' she says. I expect her to be happy, but all I see on her face is confusion. 'Pardon, young adventurer, but I don't seem to recall ever meeting you.'

I'm shocked. I turn to Ghost and see his expression suddenly drop, as if his heart was shattered in an instant.

Before he can say another word, I quickly intervene.

'Princess, surely you remember Ghost, your childhood friend?

'No, I don't.'

'Well then, perhaps you haven't fully awoken. Mayhap the journey will help improve your mood, or help recollect some old memories of your childhood?' I laugh nervously, and hope this will comfort Ghost for a short time.

She still looks confused. 'Yes, perhaps it will.'

Boon and the guards jump on their horses while I help the princess up on her personal steed. Then I mount mine while Ghost hops behind me. We set out to a cave just north from the city.

***

We ride through Jalvan Field, getting closer to our destination. As we press onward, I turn to the princess. 'I forgot to mention, Princess. Sir Kado will not be joining us.'

She replies angrily. 'It's best to leave him be until we complete this. I wish for him not to hear my voice as I sing to the holy rose.'

'Yes, someone like him isn't worthy of your melody, Princess.'

I feel Ghost tugging on my shoulder.

'Hey, Blake,' he whispers, 'did Jessica actually forget about me?'

I wonder about that myself. It's not like the princess to forget someone like Ghost. I try to comfort him. 'I believe the princess is merely pretending. I do recall a time when she was pacing around the castle, wondering if you'd ever show up. But I never told her what happened to you. I feared it would break her heart to hear the news.'

'Really? She's just upset that I didn't come back?'

'Let's not dwell on it, Ghost. We must focus on the task at hand. When we return, we'll have a private chat with her and sort this out. Also, for the moment I request you address the princess by her title. The royal guards aren't familiar with your relationship with her.'

Boon pulls back on his horse and rise beside us. 'I can understand how you feel, Ghost,' he whispers. 'I left plenty of girls heartbroken during my days as a rookie. Traveling around the world and taking on jobs, but that's the mercenary life. No girl can really tie me down.' He reaches out and pats on Ghost's back. 'Keep your head up, I'm sure the princess will give up being mad at you.'

Ghost remains silent. I do hope it's only her stubbornness that is causing her behaviour towards him. I'd hate to watch them quarrel. The thought continues to race in my head until we arrive at the cave, known as Jalvan's Scar; a place once used as a portal for the dark sorceress to summon her demonic creatures.

As we jump off our horses, the princess walks over to me. 'I wish for you and the young adventurer to remain out here for us, General.'

'Princess … surely you need more protection when entering the cave. What if there's an army waiting inside and —?'

She raises her hand, and smiles. 'I have Boon and a few of our strongest guards. I believe this shall suffice.'

I worry about the princess's idea. Most of the time I disobey her orders for her own safety, but for now I shall do as she says. 'Very well, we shall remain here until you return.'

'Thank you.'

As she walks inside with her escort, I wait for Boon to walk by me and whisper to him. 'Make a tremor strong enough to reach me out here the moment you're in danger.'

He nods. 'Understood, General.'

I watch as they disappear into the cave's darkness, and remain back with Ghost.

'Blake, what are we doing? I thought you wanted me to come along to protect Jessica.'

'I thought so, too. I don't understand what she's thinking, but I do hope this blows over soon.'

***

It's noon, and the princess is still inside the cave with her escort, while Ghost and I wait for their return. He's been pacing up and down for a while, and I can understand why. I've been leaning by the entrance with my arms crossed, worrying about the princess. Perhaps she's taking longer than usual to perform her ritual for Jalvan's good fortune inside.

But that thought is erased from my head the moment I feel a tremor from the ground. I quickly spring to action. 'Ghost, follow me inside, now!'

'What's going on?' he asks.

'I felt a tremor from the ground. I asked Boon to do that if they were in danger. And I fear that —'

We hear a loud scream coming from deep inside the cave.

'Jessica!' Ghost runs ahead of me, and uses his speed technique to hurry to her.

'Ghost, slow down!'

But he doesn't hear, and continues without me.

I keep running and running until I finally catch up to him, and see a fight going on. One guard is dead on the ground, two injured but holding their ground to protect the princess. Boon is swinging his mallet around and keeping some shadow beasts off of him, and Ghost is just standing there looking up at something. I gaze up and see a woman floating above us, laughing. I point my blade at her. 'Who are you? Why are you here?'

She looks at me with a grin across her face, but holds her tongue. Then I hear Ghost breathing in deeply, as if about to burst in anger, and shouts out, 'E'va!'

I can't believe what I hear. E'va, the shadow sorceress who plunged this kingdom into the Dark Era.

I ready myself to fight, and call out to Ghost. 'Stand your ground. We must protect the princess, and fight.'

We charge into the fury in hope of defeating E'va.

71

CHAPTER 10

Ore

I slowly open my eyes. I'm in my lab. *What was I doing? Oh, right …*

I feel exhausted, and my body refuses to move. I hear a faint noise above me, but I couldn't care less about that; all I need to do is continue my work, a way to defeat E'va.

But even that motivation isn't enough to keep my eyes open, and I slowly drift back into slumber. Visions begin to flow through my mind like a dream. It's been a while since I had visions in my sleep. Ever since I was a young boy I was able to see images, fragments of the future.

I see a cave filled with shadows of the past. Blood, and screams deep inside. They become unbearable to watch, but no matter how much I look away I can still hear the screams. I want it to stop, pleading for the visions to end.

A flood of water flows out from the cave, and with that I awaken, cold and drenched. I look up and see my wife holding a bucket with water dripping down.

'Took you long enough to get up,' she says, looking stressed.

'What happened?'

'It's Ghost. He disappeared.'

'What? Where did he go?'

She drops the bucket and falls to her knees. 'I don't know where, but I have a feeling he's gone off somewhere with the General. He wanted you to help with a request from the princess, but I said you were too exhausted to go. Ghost got excited and wanted to go, but I refused, then …'

She doesn't need to finish – I imagine Ghost sneaking out through my bedroom window.

I sit up and try to comfort Creem. 'I'm sorry for not being there for you. It should have been my responsibility to watch over him, not yours.'

'That's not all,' she says softly. 'Ever since Ghost came here he's been having dreams just as you described to me. He dreamt about being Lobia, and then he mentioned Knight, and E'va.'

My eyes widen. It has happened sooner than I expected. I need to act now, but where could Ghost be? I recall the vision I just had; a cave filled with shadows of the past: Jalvan's Scar. I go through the potions I've developed since I got back and place them in my pouch.

'Good thing you woke me up, Creem. I may have developed a potion that can suppress E'va's aura to the point of being nothing more than an ordinary mortal. I made it so it can absorb any dark magic from the target. Normally I wouldn't resort to potions, but what choice do I have against someone who's more powerful with spells and enchantments?'

I have everything packed away and ready to go. As I walk to the stairs, Creem grabs hold onto my arm.

'Please be careful. I hate to see my darling covered in wounds.' Tears fall from her eyes. I place my forehead against hers with a smile.

'Don't worry. Even if I end up injured, these potions will do the trick. I'll come back alive – and that's a promise I'm willing to fight for.'

I turn away from her and rush from my house, through the city, and past the gate. I need to move quickly before E'va makes her move. I cast a wind enchantment on my body and start running to Jalvan's Scar.

***

I arrive at the cave, pausing for a moment and sense intense aura coming from inside. It's already begun. I imagine Ghost fighting E'va with anger in his eyes. I can't allow him to go berserk again. I enter the darkness of the cave, and as I go deeper I can sense the shadows growing stronger and stronger. Then I see the fight up ahead.

Blake is down on one knee with his sword wedged to the ground; Boon is struggling to stay on his feet. A few guards are laying on the ground, motionless. I look up and see Ghost and the princess being held by E'va's dark magic. I summon my staff out and chant a spell.

'From the depths of the ocean I call forth a snake of pure water. **Sea hunter!**'

From my staff a snake made of pure water appears and charges at E'va, wrapping itself around her. It forces her to release Ghost and the princess.

Blake notices me. 'Ore, you've come!'

I stand my ground and prepare to fight. 'General, get everyone out of here. I'll deal with this sorceress myself.'

Blake gets himself up using his sword as leverage. 'What? Are you certain about this?'

'I'm positive, now go!'

He carries the princess out, but as usual Ghost chooses the worst time to argue. 'I'm not leaving you here alone, Ore.'

'I've got no time to argue with you. Now, do as I say.'

He presses his head against mine. 'She took us both down when we last fought. If we all fight together, we'll stand a chance.'

Oh, how I hate his stubbornness.

I step back and raise my hand to his face. 'We can talk about this later. Now, **sleep!**' I click my fingers, and watch him struggle to keep his eyes open.

When he falls asleep, I call out to Boon. 'Get Ghost out of here!'

He walks over and picks him up. 'Try not to get yourself killed, Ore.'

As he runs out, I focus my attention on E'va, who looks bored.

'How touching to risk your own skin just to let these mortals live. Such a typical sight to behold on someone who'll die in the end.'

She lowers herself to the ground, breaking free from my spell. I bring out a potion and toss it at her. But E'va casts her black shards and destroys the bottle.

'Well, I've overestimated you. To think an immortal would use such a worthless little trick. It doesn't matter what you do, really. My plan has already been set in motion long before you came here.' As she walks over to me, E'va steps onto the puddle of my potion and in an instant it wraps around her, and begins to generate heat.

I relax a little, and watch her struggle to break free.

'You fell for it. It took me some time to perfect it. A potion that can turn into a slime the moment it comes into contact with dark magic. Struggle all you want, it won't let go of you anytime soon.'

E'va continues to struggle, and starts to concentrate on her aura. 'Don't think this trick will contain me, Little Wizard.'

The slime starts to swell up and boil. I don't know how long it'll hold her, but I need to act now before it's too late. I reach for another potion, but E'va breaks free by releasing her aura on the slime, forcing it to burst and scatter. Some of it goes on my face and hair. My flesh burns and I scream out in pain, trying to get it off. I cast an ice spell to freeze the remains and pull them off of me.

When I return my attention to E'va, there's a shocked look on her face. 'Silver over black hair?' she mutters. 'A disguise …?'

My enchantment must have been broken by the slime! As she takes a step forward, I quickly chant, 'Darkness loom over my enemy and curse them for eternity. **Black shroud!**'

E'va's eyes widen as shadowy mist launches from my sleeves, covering her completely. It's been too long since I last used it; it's a spell that drains too much from the caster. I let my guard down and take a moment to recover, only to hear E'va scream, '**Black serpent!**'

A black snake rushes out from the mist and bites me in the left shoulder. I reach for it and try to rip it out but its fangs are already deep into my skin. If I keep on pulling, it might rip my arm off.

Falling to my knees and feeling numb, I watch the black mist fade away, revealing E'va's angry expression. 'I should have realised sooner. Everything you said to me puzzled my mind. How you're able to know everything there is about me is finally clear. I can see the same colour eyes as my own. The same colour hair as my own. I can't believe all this time you were alive, and fighting against me!'

I can feel her emotions run wild. The black snake lifts me in the air and slams me to the ground.

'Please stop this, E'va,' I plead.

But that only angers her more. Her aura starts to run out of control, and her voice only grows louder and louder. 'You promised to stand by my side no matter what! Why have you sided with those worthless mortals after everything they did to us? Answer me, O'va!'

It's been so long since I heard my true name from her.

I begin to lose consciousness as the snake's fangs crush my arm. I'm losing all feeling in my body, and my vision starts to blur.

Is this the end for me? Have I actually lost to my own sister?

I whisper softly to myself. 'Forgive me, Creem.'

I can still hear E'va screaming out of control, but then I hear another voice shouting out.

'**Ultimate … strike!**'

Through the blurry vision I see E'va get hit by someone. I can tell who it is from the technique – Ghost. That idiot came back.

It's too late for me. I can't feel anything, and my mind falls into darkness.

CHAPTER 11

Ore

Darkness, emptiness. A void.

This runs through my mind as I float in the eternal sea of shadows. I can't see, nor can I tell if I'm moving, but what I do know is this.

I'm dead. Killed by my own sister, who didn't spare a thought about losing her brother.

In a way, I lost her the moment she went insane. The lust to kill, the intent to enslave the dead, and to burn all of life for a single goal. I wish I had the strength to beat her, but alas my power couldn't compare to her own. There's nothing I can do but drift aimlessly in this void until I lose my mind.

My only regret is that I'll never see Creem again, and that she will mourn over my death. I can imagine her face covered in tears. I wish I could just come back, but it's impossible even for an immortal to return.

Forgive me, Creem.

At that moment I hear someone crying. The sound grows louder until suddenly I regain my sight, and through the void I see a ray of light. It warms my soul, and I find myself awake from the bright light of the sun.

Then I hear, 'Please, Ore. Please come back to me. Don't let the void swallow you whole.'

I turn my head and see Creem crying over me. 'Creem? How did I …?'

She opens her eyes. 'Thank goodness, you're alive! I thought I lost you.'

I look around. There's a fountain in the middle of an area filled with flowers and plants. 'Is this the castle garden? How did I get here?'

'I was worried you wouldn't return, so I decided to head to Jalvan's Scar and save you from your demise. When I arrived, everyone was outside but you. I feared the worse, and then Ghost woke up and went back in. I tried to follow him, but he was too fast for me to keep up. When I arrived, I saw you two unconscious. There was so much blood, and I couldn't feel your pulse, nor your aura.'

Tears flow from Creem's eyes again, although she's doing her best to dry them.

'I'm alive, aren't I? So there's no need to cry. It makes me feel sad to watch a beautiful forest rose cry her eyes out.'

Though my words are soothing, she doesn't calm down. Creem clutches my robe and looks at me with her frightening eyes still filled with tears. 'Don't try to compliment me at a time like this. You are never to go against your sister alone. Is that clear?'

I start to shrivel in fear and slowly nod. 'Sure, I promise not to risk my life again, sweetie.' I look away from Creem, and try to forget seeing her scary side. Then I tell her what I heard from E'va. 'She said it. She said my name.'

'Did she actually?'

'Yes, yet she still tried to kill me, thanks to my own error with the potions. They weren't enough to stop her. I tried to use a spell she's well familiar with, but in the end it only made things worse.'

'O'va …' Creem starts stroking my head. 'Please don't blame yourself. You said there's no way of saving her. That nothing could bring her out from her own madness.'

'Even so …' I try to hold my tears, but I just can't. 'I thought to try and restrain E'va, then reveal myself to her so she could snap out of it. But I hesitated when she began to figure it out, and so I attacked her. If only I made that slime strong enough, I could have …'

I wish there was a way to help my sister, but it'll never happen. E'va has fallen into deep despair from the pain she felt the moment we came to this realm four hundred years ago.

'O'va, please don't cry. Maybe this will help?' Creem starts humming a soothing melody; an ancient song that was once used by a race that went extinct during the Dark Era. I start to feel calm, and my mind begins to clear up all negative thoughts. I remain silent, listening to Creem humming away happily. It reminds me of when we first met. I was alone and in pain, but she healed all of my wounds and calmed the anger in my heart with this melody.

But it is soon cut short by a disturbing voice.

'Well, seeing the princess's adviser in tears is a rare sight, indeed. It's a shame that it won't last that long. And I must say, seeing those sections of black hair amongst the silver is certainly a surprise, including those red eyes of yours. If you ask me, they seem quite frightening.'

I slowly rise from Creem's lap to face a man with a smirk on his face. 'Hello, Kado. How awful it is to see you again.'

'Oh, Ore. How rude of you to address the Reborn Knight. Do you wish for me to revive my mistress?' He places his hand on the hilt of his dagger, ready to draw it out.

'Is there a reason why you're here, Kado?' Creem asks.

He brushes his short red hair back, and looks her up and down. 'Well, I felt the need to set my eyes on something stunning and beautiful, which brought me to this garden hoping to see the princess. But I found you. Seeing you in your lovely medical uniform makes me want to injure myself, just to have some quality time with you.'

He's starting to cross a line that may lead to the end of his life. I couldn't care less about who he is; anyone who tries to flirt with my

Creem will surely die by my hands. Just as I am about to get up, I feel a grip on my arm and notice a vine wrapped around it.

I look at Creem, who appears to be only annoyed by his compliment. 'Please refrain from saying such disgusting words, Kado. Or else the next thing that'll come out of your mouth will be a pool of your own blood.'

He slowly backs away from us. 'Hey, now. I was only joking. I'd be a fool to try and make a move on you, Creem. After all, you're married to the wisest wizard of Jalvan. What woman wouldn't want a man with such incredible power? Anyway, I'll go ahead and take my leave. I hope you feel better now, O'v—I mean Ore.'

I stare at Kado as he walks away. 'He must have overheard us.'

'It's my fault for saying your name. I can't believe that snake managed to conceal his aura.'

I reach out to her with my injured arm, trying to resist the pain. 'Don't blame yourself. We shouldn't focus on him at all. We need to come up with a way to deal with E'va. She told me that nothing we do will stop her plan, and I'm positive it involves Ghost.'

'You're right, but for now you should rest that arm. Don't go moving it or else the wound will reopen.' Gently grabbing my arm, Creem starts healing it with magic.

'Yes, dear. I need a break after how much I went through just to stop my sister.'

A scream comes from inside the castle.

'What the hell was that?' I shout.

Two guards come rushing past us. Creem calls out to them. 'Guards, what's all the commotion about?'

'The adventurer that we took in after the incident in Jalvan's Scar went insane and started running around the castle.'

'By any chance did the adventurer say anything that made him go crazy?' I ask him.

'The report mentioned him shouting out "Demons!" at a few other guards, which lead to them pursuing him,' the guard replies.

I clench my right hand. 'That moron thinks he's dead!'

'I beg your pardon, adviser?' asks the other guard.

'This isn't the first time that idiot has thought he was dead. One time we went overboard in his training, and after a few days of rest he started going on about being in the afterlife. He thought I was a demon in disguise. Where is he right now?'

'He was last seen heading straight to the castle tower.'

'Oh, boar dung. Something tells me he may be—'

There's another loud scream from the top of the castle.

'That sounded like the princess,' says Creem. She starts running into the castle.

I try to follow her, but my shoulder aches and forces me to walk. 'Guards, take me to the adventurer's room. We'll meet up with Creem there.'

I just hope that idiot doesn't go running off while I'm there.

CHAPTER 12

Ghost

The village is on fire. Black flames engulf every building in sight, and the dark mist looms all around me, corrupting the ground, turning it into ash. I hear the screams of the victims as they slowly die, the roars of the fairy elf warriors charging at me. They swoop with their sharp leaf blades and try to cut me down. I dodge their attacks and cut their heads off with a swing from my blade.

'These weaklings are meant to help us achieve our goals? I wish not to question your plan, Mistress, but I have to ask. Why are we here?'

My mistress appears from the ground. 'I believe they hold something that will benefit us. Something that was once used during the ancient times.' She embraces me, staring right into my eyes. 'What I'm about to tell you stays between you, me, and my brother.'

My eyes widen, and I lean closer to hear her secret. 'I shall never speak a word of it.'

'Good. What we're looking for is an orb with the blood of a lijin sealed within. With it, and my blood of a shajin, we can create something wonderful. Something that shall grant your wish – a flow of aura that can destroy anything, even those who are impossible to kill. God-like powers.'

'Your wisdom and power never cease to amaze me, Mistress. It is truly an honour to serve under you.'

She blushes. 'Oh, come now. Save the compliments for when we acquire the blood we need.' She gasps and looks around, worry in her eyes. 'O'va … His aura suddenly disappeared. Knight, forget our objective. Find O'va.'

'Right away, Mistress.'

We split up and search through the black flames. I destroy any debris that stands in my way, and call out for O'va.

I come across a temple. When I search inside, I see before me an orb glowing brightly. It could be what my mistress is looking for. I don't want to disobey her order, but the temptation of achieving her other goal is too great. I take a deep breath and slowly approach it. Just as I'm able to grab hold of the orb, the roof cracks and collapses on top of me.

Everything goes fuzzy. I lose all feeling to my body, but my mind lingers. I can hear the sound of the temple falling apart. The last thing I see is the orb shining brightly, taunting me.

Am I being punished for disobeying her? Am I going to die like this?

All I can do now is close my eyes and await my soul to drift into the afterlife, and be reborn.

***

I sit up and start screaming. Someone immediately punches me in the face.

I lift myself back up, and with my hand on my nose, I start yelling. 'What the hell was that for, Ore? You shouldn't go punching someone after they have a nightmare.'

'The only person here who needs to understand what they shouldn't do is you, Ghost. Who the hell runs around the castle like a madman thinking he's dead?'

We stare at each other like angry dogs, but then I notice something. His eyes look different, and his hair looks like it's had black ink splashed on it. 'What happened to you?'

He closes his eyes and scratches his hair with his right hand. 'Well … I was thinking of changing my appearance. It has been like this for centuries.'

I squint at his hair again. It looks dyed, and I don't buy the fact that it's been centuries since he last changed it. Before I can say anything else to him, I start to feel very weak and fall back down on the bed. 'Where am I?'

Creem walks over and places her hands above me, casting a healing spell. 'You're resting in one of the castle's rooms. You were out cold when I arrived at Jalvan's Scar, and Ore was in a critical condition. But I've done my part and treated you both.' She finishes and puts her hands behind her back. 'There, that should help you recover. I notice that your body suffers from a strain which causes it to lock your muscles, preventing them from moving correctly.'

'Well, that's my weakness, alright. Every time I use my ultimate techniques, my body starts to shift depending on what I'm doing. With my own aura it allows me to speed my heart rate for speed and doubles my strength, but the side effect is a shock to my body. It's little insane, but it works well for me.'

I lay back down on my bed and stretch my body in the sheets, getting myself comfortable.

'It's actually the first time I've heard you admitting how insane your fighting style is, Ghost,' Ore says. 'Like a man being poisoned by his own aura, just to bear the strength to fight.'

'Do you have to use your wise quotes, Ore? I'm starting to get sick of them.'

'One must never doubt the—'

Before Ore finishes boring me to death, the door opens. Blake and Jessica enter.

'Ah, I see you're awake. How are you feeling?' Blake asks me.

I jump out of bed and stretch my right arm in the air. 'As good as any other great adventurer.'

'I'm relieved to hear that. I wish I could have done more, but it can't be helped against someone far stronger than me.'

I place my hands on my hips. 'There's no need to worry about it, Blake. I am reckless after all, so it would be hard to watch my back.'

'I can agree with that from experience,' Ore says with a whistle.

'Pardon the interruption, but may I ask you some questions, adventurer?' Jessica is staring at me. She appears to be blushing a little.

'Sure ... go ahead.'

She takes a deep breath. 'Do you recall seeing anything while you explored the castle?'

'What do you mean by—?'

'There isn't anything you need to worry about, princess,' Ore interrupts. 'Ghost normally doesn't remember anything of that sort after he passes out.'

'Oh, good. Then I shall forgive him for storming into my room without permission.'

'Well … I remember running up somewhere, then I saw something pink, and frilly? The rest is fuzzy.' I notice Jessica's face turning red. Ore smacks his hand to his face, shaking his head. 'Did I say something wrong?'

I brace myself for what's going to come, but Jessica takes another deep breath. 'I'll pretend those words never came out of your mouth, and move on to more important matters.' She steps forward commandingly. 'I wish to know why you act as if we know each other. Have we met somewhere a long time ago? Or were you once part of my royal guard? If so it would explain your devotion to protect me within Jalvan's Scar.'

Jessica keeps coming closer and closer to me, asking so many questions that I can't answer because she won't let me speak, until I finally yell, 'What's wrong with me protecting someone I love?'

My voice echoes around the room, then silence falls. Jessica's eyes widen.

Blake steps forward and places his hand on her shoulder. 'Princess, please. If this is some way of expressing your anger towards Ghost, then I suggest you cease with this childish act. Surely you still care for him despite how long he's kept you waiting.'

'Hold on …' Creem says, surprised. 'Ghost and the princess have a relationship? Darling, do you know anything about this?'

'It's the first I ever heard Ghost mention his sweetheart's name,' Ore says. 'I recall him mentioning a love before we arrived in The Capital, but nothing else.'

I look at them. 'Wait … I never told you guys?'

They both yell, 'No, you haven't!'

I smile nervously, scratching my head, and turn back to Jessica. Her head is hanging low; then, she starts to giggle and lifts her head back up, covering her mouth. She backs away, brushing Blake's hand off her shoulder.

'Why would I be in love with such a reckless little boy like you? You don't seem to be like any standard type of adventurer, let alone be someone I would fall in love with. I bet you were raised poorly by your parents, with no care to correct their child's imagination.'

My eyes widen, and tears slowly flow out. Her words echo in my mind, and my heart begins to ache. I hear Blake yelling at her. 'Princess, that's going too far, even if you are upset!'

I lower my head as they argue, and start to feel something flaring up inside me; the same feeling I had when I was fighting E'va. I can hear my heart beat slowly, more quietly, until I can hear it no longer.

Voices echo around me; they keep getting louder and louder. I try to cover my ears, but the voices won't stop. I refuse to believe she has forgotten about me, I refuse to believe what she said.

But as my mind snaps and everything goes silent, I hear one voice.

'I've warned you. She has forgotten about you.'

I scream out in anger, then grab my sword and throw it at Jessica's left side. It flies by her shoulder and straight through the wall. She looks scared.

Blake quickly grabs both my arms and restrains me. 'Ghost, what are you thinking? Trying to harm the princess? You shouldn't resort to anger that way. What would your father say if he—?'

'Shut up, Blake! I don't want to hear it.'

Then Ore steps in and grabs my shoulder. 'Ghost, calm down. Do not allow that anger of yours to gain control …' He gasps, as if he senses something inside of me. Then he mumbles softly, 'E'va.'

As he mentions her name, I hear E'va's voice. *'Run. Grab your sword and escape while you still can. Do not allow them to apprehend you.'*

I take a step forward but feel Ore's hand gripping onto my shoulder, and Blake holding onto my arms tightly. 'Don't listen. Do not heed her words, Ghost. Please, calm down and let me help you.'

'Quickly now. He will not help you. Only I can. I'm the only one who understand your pain.' Then she screams. *'Now! Strike him!'*

I use my aura to break free from Blake, and punch Ore in the face, freeing myself from his hold. Creem summons vines from her back, but I dodge them by using my acceleration technique. I grab my sword and run out of the room. As I'm running through the hallway, I recall Jessica laughing at me, and know that E'va was right all along. I should have trusted her, but Ore prevented me from doing that.

I need to find E'va.

CHAPTER 13

Ghost

As I make my way out of the castle, incredible pain erupts in my body. I fall to my knees, coughing up blood. Dammit, I've pushed my body too much. But I can't stop now. I need to find E'va.

I force my body up, and continue running. As I'm heading to the city gate, I hear E'va. *'What are you doing? You're heading over to—'*

I answer using my thoughts. *'I'm trying to get to the city's entrance. If I'm quick enough, I'll be able to—'*

But before I can finish the thought, I see a group of guards barricading the entrance.

'Well, I could have warned you sooner, but you fail to let me finish explaining the situation. Now, go north and keep going until I order you to halt.'

I listen to her and make my way north. *'Hold on, why are you directing me into the military district?'*

'Just do as I say and we'll both make it out of here alive.'

Another group of guards appear behind me and start giving chase. I knew this was the wrong way to go; at this rate, I'll be captured.

Another guard stands up ahead. 'Halt, don't take another step!'

I stop and pull my sword out, ready to battle my way out of this despite how exhausted my body is.

The guards behind me keep their distance, bringing out their magical rifles.

'I don't want to start any trouble,' I call to them. 'All I want to do is leave the city.'

'We received orders from the general himself to capture you,' one of the guards behind me yells back. 'Lower your weapon and come peacefully. Or else we'll take you by force.'

I don't seem to have any option but to fight. I ready myself to sprint at the guards and strike them with my blade before they can fire their rifles. But my body won't move at all, and I don't think I can do another ultimate technique without passing out. I call out to E'va in my mind.

'What do I do now?'

But I hear nothing.

'Don't do anything stupid. There's no need to make a single move,' says the guard in front of me. She's standing alone with a smile across her face. Though I can't see the top half of her head because of her hat, I feel like I know that voice.

As I'm weighing my options, another voice comes from behind me. 'My, oh my. What seems to be the trouble, boys?' Coming through the group is a man with his dagger out and resting on his left shoulder. 'I assume that this little runt is the one the general informed us about?'

I'm not sure who this guy is, but I can tell he's a cocky adventurer. One of those types who think they are too important for anyone.

'Yes, this is the adventurer that the general wishes to be captured,' a guard says. 'With you here, Kado, we'll be able to apprehend him in mere seconds.'

Kado starts laughing. 'Well, of course. There isn't anyone alive who can take on the Reborn Knight.'

He slowly approaches with his dagger pointing at me. I ready myself to use whatever strength and aura I have left in my body. Then the female guard walks past me, her smile down to a frown.

'I beg your pardon? Did my ears deceive me, or do you claim to be a knight from the Dark Era?'

Kado flexes his muscles. 'Why, yes I am,' he boasts. 'The very same knight who is reborn by the power of the dark sorceress's magic.'

Hold on – this guy is the Reborn Knight Ore mentioned? I'm starting to feel nervous; I remember Ore telling me how dangerous the knight is. But then I feel a dark chill coming from the female guard.

'How dare you?' she says angrily. 'How dare you claim to be my knight? Begone, and never say such disrespectful words. **Black shroud!**'

A cloud of darkness appears from the female guard, engulfing Kado and the rest of the guards standing behind him. That's when the female guard removes her hat. It's E'va.

I'm completely shocked to see her in disguise. 'But, how? When?'

She grabs my hand and pulls me close to her. 'There will be a time for me to explain how I got in. For now, stay close and we shall escape.'

I feel nervous this close to E'va. Her chest presses against me. I feel blood start to trickle from my nose.

'Um … can't we just climb over the city's wall?' I ask, holding my nose tightly.

'No, this is much faster.' She rests her head on my shoulder. 'I truly miss this feeling.'

I don't know how to feel about this; she's getting a bit too close for comfort. But then I look down and see that we are sinking into the ground; as if our shadow is swallowing us whole.

'Just relax and allow the darkness to take you away from this place.'

As we completely sink into the ground, my vision goes black and I hear nothing.

***

I open my eyes, gasping for air. I'm in Javan's Field. E'va stands with her right hand on a tree, staring off into the distance. I wonder what's on her mind, but then she speaks.

 'I recall a time when we used to gaze on a quiet field. I would be in your arms as you stroked my hair. I always asked if you would remain by my side and follow my orders, and you would always say yes. I truly enjoyed the time we spent together.'

But her gentle gaze turns dark as her eyes close. Her grip tightens on the tree, and its leaves start to wither and fall. 'I wish I could go back to those memories, but fate has a twisted sense of humour. I ordered you not to go after the orb with the lijin blood sealed inside. I ordered you to find my brother, and yet you went after that orb.'

A chill rolls down my spine; I'm afraid of her now. Her eyes open and she stares directly at me, sheer anger flowing within them.

'But I only wished to kill two birds with one stone,' I say, surprising myself. 'To find the lijin's blood and your brother.' I don't know why I said that; I was never there.

E'va walks over, her eyes fixed on mine. 'It's because of your action that you died. I thought I was left alone. I thought I lost everything. I wrestled you out of the rubble, only to look into your eyes and see no life coming from it. I tried desperately to reclaim you, but I only obtained your fragment.'

I don't want to listen to this.

'I was never there!' I shout. 'I dreamt that moment before, but I wasn't even born. What the hell does this all mean? Why have you been after me? And most importantly, who the hell am I?'

My words snap E'va from her anger. She drops to her knees, looking at me sorrowfully. 'Forgive me, I didn't mean to say those things. I was so happy to have you back that I reverted back into the past. It's not your fault – it was your first life that caused me so much grief.'

'What do you mean by first life? Can you explain to me, E'va?' I walk over to the withered tree. 'Ore kept something from me, which he said he'd help me with but never did. And you seem to know a lot more about this than he does. So, I'll ask again – who am—?'

As I turn, a blade is shoved through my chest. E'va has her eyes closed, a black dagger dripping with dark aura in her hand.

'There's no need to worry. This will help you. You will feel nothing during the ritual we shall embark on. Your soul shall reform into a body of pure darkness. Then, and only then, you will receive the answers you seek. My Knight.'

CHAPTER 14

Blake

It's been two hours since Ghost stormed out of the castle. I've ordered every available guard to barricade the city gate, including the docks. With every corner of the city on high alert, there has been no sign of him.

I pace up and down the bridge between the city centre and the castle, my nerves running wild. I pull out my com crystal and speak clearly into it. 'Has there been any sighting of the adventurer I described?'

'Gate team reporting. No sign of the adventurer, sir.'

'Dock team reporting. There has been no sighting around here either, sir. We went ahead and asked the residents, but nothing so far.'

I clench my fist and slam it against a pillar. 'Stay vigilant! There's no telling how he could escape.'

I continue to wait impatiently, feeling stressed about the situation. How could the princess forget about Ghost after all the times I heard her yelling his name as a child? Even going so far as tormenting me with tears and pranks to make me take her over to his home. But now, I'm starting to believe it's something else.

Have her duties erased her memories of him? Or perhaps something has happened to her while I was busy with my own duties. I can't put my finger on it, but I must focus on finding him.

I raise my com crystal. 'This is General Blake, requesting to speak with Guild Master Vanger.'

He immediately replies. 'General, Vanger here. I was about to call you on a situation my men are having. The city guards are refusing to let them back in after coming back from a mission. You care to tell me what's going on?'

'There isn't time to explain the full story. Right now, I want you to send some of your scouts around the city and find a young adventurer with brown hair and a long sword on his back.'

'That's not a very detailed description, but if my men report something I'll make sure you hear it first. I'll have the fastest team scout the city while the others outside search around the outer wall.'

I place my crystal into my pouch and hope to hear from them soon. Knowing Vanger's scout team, they will certainly find Ghost no matter where he's hiding. I take a minute to collect myself from my madness and lean against the pillar, my hand on my helmet.

'Has there been any word about Ghost, General?' I turn and see Ore coming from the castle entrance. He approaches me and gently bows his head. 'Forgive me for failing to keep Ghost at ease. I only wished to tell him about his condition, but I feared E'va would use that to her advantage. Either way, she has beaten me.'

'Do not blame yourself, Ore. You did all you could do. Whatever you know about Ghost, you did it to protect him from whatever fate has in store for him. Where is Creem?'

'She went out to find Ghost outside the city walls in case he escaped. I would have gone with her, but you know her attitude towards the injured.'

'Well, I've received no sighting of him. Vanger sent his scouts to search, including the outer wall. I just hope that evil sorceress didn't get to him before we did.'

I fear E'va may twist his mind and make him into a warrior of destruction. *Though, if you ask me, Ghost is already like that – just not evil, and never intending to cause harm to those around him.* As I ponder, a report comes in from my com crystal. I quickly grab it from my pouch.

'General, this is Vanger. My scouts reported some magical barrier outside the military district. After they dispelled it, they found some guards unconscious, along with Kado. I arrived here myself to examine the bodies. Unfortunately, the guards are dead, and Kado is barely alive.'

'What? Do you know the cause of their deaths?'

'I'm uncertain. We did detect a strange aura in the area, but we can't tell what type. Also, the guards have black marks all over their bodies, and Kado only has a few less than the rest.'

I don't understand what's going on. First, Ghost disappears, and now this.

Before I can finish speaking with Vanger, Ore comes close and speaks clear into the crystal.

'Vanger, it's Ore. Take Kado to the medical centre right away. Those black marks are caused by a deadly spell from the Dark Era. Be cautious of the area and have your scouts expand their search around Jalvan Field.'

'Understood, Ore. I'll get my best men to head out right away.'

I put my crystal away and turn my attention to Ore. 'Why do we need to search Jalvan Field? How could Ghost have gotten out there?'

'He couldn't have snuck out alone. Those black marks are E'va's doing, which means she got to him first.'

'What? She already has him? Then we must hurry. I'll order the guards to break from barricade formation and charge into the field.'

Before I can give the order, Ore grabs my arm. 'Terrible idea, General. If we include the city guards, it will only cause more casualties. It's best to have some of Vanger's scouts for backup. They can handle E'va using their speed to dodge her spells.'

'You're right. Then I'll head out myself to deal with this mess.'

'I won't allow that. I'll go with you.'

'But you're injured!'

He lets go of my arm and clenches his fist, leaking out an electric aura. 'I refuse to sit idly by and let Ghost be consumed by darkness. I didn't save him just so he can be a puppet.'

I can see the spark in Ore's eyes. A man determined to go to war for a friend. I nod, and we both set out to find him, before his soul is swallowed by the void.

***

We charge through the fields to the east, hoping to find Ghost before E'va's darkness consumes his mind. As we press onward, Ore suddenly stops and looks to the north. 'I sense Creem's aura. She's in trouble,' he says. 'Follow me.'

We change direction and continue north of the fields. Just as I can feel a disrupting flow of aura, I hear a voice from my com crystal.

'General, this is Scout Team Seventeen. We found the adventurer. He's just south-east of Jalvan's Scar, fighting the medical chief, Creem. What do we do, sir?'

'Provide support for Creem. Ore and I are currently heading to your position. Do whatever it takes to subdue the adventurer.'

'Understood. We will—' The scout's voice cuts off.

'Scout Team? Respond! What's happening?'

No answer.

I hurry as fast as I can, but then something comes hurtling towards us. Ore jumps in front of me and casts a spell to slow it down until it's close enough for him to catch in his right arm.

I can't believe my eyes. It was Creem who was hurled towards us. Ore gently places her down with her head on his lap.

'Creem? What happened? Where is Ghost?' I notice her wings are out. Having known Creem for so long, I'm aware that these wings are typically hidden by her magic; only visible when she's in battle, or weakened. They look as if they've been torn up by a sword.

Her eyes open and her wings start to flap, but that only makes her grunt in pain. *Damn, what could have gone through Ghost's mind to do such a terrible thing?*

'Don't move, Creem,' Ore pleads. 'You're too injured to fight.'

Creem tries to stand up, but I force her down gently. 'Please rest, Creem. We shall take it from here.'

'General …' she says, then loses consciousness.

'General!'

I turn around and see three scout troops approaching us.

'What's the situation with the adventurer? And where is your squad captain?'

'Our captain has ordered us to retreat, and has taken on the adventurer alone.'

'I want you three to take Creem back to the city. She needs medical treatment.'

'Yes, General.' The scout team carries Creem and hurries back to the city. Just as they are out of sight, something else crashes in front of us. Only this time it is Ghost, the squad captain in his arms. Ghost throws the scout captain to his right, the man covered in blood.

'Ghost!' I call out to him.

But he doesn't respond.

'Ghost,' I try again. 'Why are you doing this? Has E'va's words corrupted your mind? I know you'd never step down this path. Lay down your weapon and surrender. I wish not to harm you.'

He starts laughing like a madman, and points his finger at me with a grin across his face.

'Is that all?' Ghost says. 'Do you truly think your words can reach him? Even if they do, he would never listen after everything you kept from him.'

A dark bolt shoots from his finger. I block the attack but suffer an aftershock.

'Blake, that isn't Ghost,' Ore shouts. 'Don't listen to a word he says.'

'Silence!' Ghost shouts, and raises his hand. Black vines burst from the ground and wrap around us. 'You've said enough, O'va. And now you will suffer for your betrayal.'

I struggle to break free, but the vines are too strong. I watch as Ore rises up and bolts of lightning strike him multiple times.

I have no choice. To save us from demise, I have to resort to my trump card. I channel my aura to the centre of my body. Allowing it to grow and become unstable. Then I shout out from the top of my lungs.

'Ultimate … explosion!'

My aura explodes, causing Ghost to take damage and shattering the vines, freeing us.

'Ore!' I shout. 'Are you alright?' My ears ring loudly, and I can barely hear my own voice.

Faintly I hear him reply. 'I'm fine, Blake. A reckless move, but a wise one nonetheless.'

I stand up and face Ghost, who is struggling to get up off the ground. 'Damn you, mortal. You will pay for this.' He falls back and a shadow flows out of him. It takes a new form. Appearing above him now is the evil sorceress, E'va.

'To think I would be harmed by an attack like that,' she says, her expression happy. 'No matter. I've had my fun in that shell. My objective was achieved long before you two even found me.'

From her right hand appears a flame of pure light.

'What is that?' I ask.

E'va laughs as she raises it in the air. 'Why, it's the very thing you came for. The soul of the little boy you deceived.'

My eyes widen, and I gasp. We're too late to save Ghost. I take a step forward but fall to my knees, exhausted from the technique I used.

'Why,' I ask angrily. 'Why must you do this? And what have we done to deceive Ghost? I swore to him that I'd protect him when he was a child.'

E'va floats down to the ground. 'Don't bother trying to convince him. He's already become loyal to me. And unlike that princess, I will make sure he's taken care of.' She smiles. 'Speaking of the princess, I suggest you go see her. In case she has collapsed.' E'va laughs as she disappears underground.

What does she mean? Has something happened to the princess? I want to rush to her aid but my body refuses to move.

Instead I watch as Ore slowly approaches Ghost's body, shedding tears and crying out into the wilderness.

I can't believe my own failure to protect him. I said to myself that I would never allow the darkness to consume him, but I couldn't even keep my word.

I lower my head to the ground, my thoughts focused on one man.

'Forgive me, Drake. I failed you. I failed to protect your son.'

ACKNOWLEDGMENTS

A shout out to the cover designer, Zac Coverdale.

The teachers from the Melbourne Polytechnic Campus in Prahran who taught me for years, building my skills for fictional writing.

My classmates who have given me helpful feedback on my work.

My friends who have given me encouragement to publish.

And lastly, Busybird Publishing for helping me construct this book and bringing it into reality.

ABOUT THE AUTHOR

Jake Triulcio is a writer and a kitchenhand in a pub.

His debut novella, *The Knight: Dark Era*, is Volume I of a planned series that will further explore the world of Levda and its cast of magical and mysterious characters.

Jake was born in Australia and has an Italian background, and is the youngest of four siblings. When he's not building the lore of his fantasy worlds, Jake enjoys gaming or hanging out at the same pub he works in.

www.ingramcontent.com/pod-product-compliance
Lightning Source LLC
Chambersburg PA
CBHW030839200726
48285CB00007B/2488